With special thanks to Catherine Diaz, Dental Hygienist,
for her help in preparing the tooth-brushing chart.

Text copyright © 1992 by Carol Carrick

Illustration copyright © 1992 by Lisa McCue

Library of Congress Cataloging-in-Publication Data

Carrick, Carol.
Norman fools the tooth fairy / by Carol Carrick; illustrated by
Lisa McCue.
p.   cm.
Summary: When Norman tries to trick the tooth fairy by slipping her a
fake tooth, he is surprised by a visit from the tooth monster.
[1. Tooth Fairy—Fiction.   2. Teeth—Fiction.]   I. McCue, Lisa,
ill. II. Title.
PZ7.C2344No   1991

[E]—dc20   91-16634
CIP
AC

ISBN 0-590-42240-5
12 11 10 9 8 7 6 5 4 3 2 1   2 3 4 5 6/9
Printed in the U.S.A.   36

First Scholastic printing, April 1992

Designed by Adrienne M. Syphrett

The art for this book was painted
with acrylics, color inks,
and watercolors.

To Sally Ward
who has a perfect smile
– C.C.

To Peanut
with love, Mommy
– L.M.

Norman was the only kid in his class
who hadn't lost a baby tooth. One was sort
of loose now. Instead of finishing his
worksheet, Norman wiggled the tooth with
his finger.

Later, while his teacher, Miss Harp, read them a story, Norman waggled the tooth with his tongue. How else was he going to get a tooth to put under his pillow for the tooth fairy?

His friends gave him lots of advice. "I tied a string around my loose tooth," said Toby. "Then I tied the other end to a doorknob, and my sister slammed the door."

Norman winced.

"My dad pulled mine out," said Matt, "with his pliers."

Norman shuddered, but he admired the empty space between their teeth when they smiled. It showed that the tooth fairy had already paid them a visit.

"Try biting into an apple," said Sarah, "or eat lots of caramels."

Norman didn't have any caramels, but he did have a piece of licorice in his lunch bag.

Norman tried chewing on the licorice for a while. But nothing happened. Then he stuck it over his tooth. "Look at me now," he said.

"Hey!" said Toby. "Norman lost his front tooth."

When Norman ate the licorice off, everyone laughed.

That night Norman stuck some licorice
on his tooth again and smiled at himself in
the mirror. He looked wonderful, as though
a tooth were really missing.

It gave him an idea. He fooled his
friends. Why not fool the tooth fairy?
Maybe she would think his tooth really
fell out. But the tooth fairy would want
to see it.

Norman searched the bathroom for something like a tooth. At last he broke off a tooth-sized chip of soap. "Perfect!" he said, and wrapped it in toilet paper. Then, when Norman went to bed, he stuck the fake tooth under his pillow and turned out the light.

Norman tossed and turned, waiting for the tooth fairy to come. What would she be like, he wondered. Maybe she would be a pretty lady in a sparkling gown, looking for lost teeth.

"Hey, tooth fairy!" he would call to her. "Here's one."

Norman felt for the soap chip under his pillow. It was very small, and it was hard to find. The tooth fairy might not see it.

He wrapped lots of toilet paper around the fake tooth and marked it NORMAN'S TOOTH. It made a big lump under his pillow. Now she couldn't miss it.

Norman lay in bed, waiting. Soon the
tooth fairy would float into his room with
a bag of money.

After a while he began to worry. How
does she know when someone's tooth falls
out? Does the tooth fairy just go from
house to house, looking under pillows?

Norman got out of bed and made a sign
with his crayons. TOOTH UNDER HERE
it said. An arrow pointed to his pillow just
to be sure.

It must be very late, Norman thought. Maybe she wasn't going to come. Once, he even dozed off. But he woke with a start and checked the tooth under his pillow. He hoped that, somehow, a quarter had taken its place. But no—the lump of toilet paper and soap was still there.

What did the tooth fairy do with all those teeth? Norman wondered. She must want them for something special. Maybe she made them into key chains.

Now Norman saw a light come through his window.
It was growing larger. He peeked between his closed eyelids,
hoping for a glimpse of the pretty lady. What he saw did not
look like a tooth fairy to Norman. It looked more like a monster
with baby teeth hanging from her necklace. It was a tooth
monster coming toward his bed.

"Teeth!" the tooth monster yelled. "I want teeth!"
Little helpers were following behind her. "Teeth!" they
chanted, waving pliers. "Gimmee teeth!"
"There's a kid with a whole mouthful," one of them
screeched. "Let's get him!"

"Wait!" Norman was so excited that he swallowed the licorice. "There aren't any teeth here—honest!" he said. "I was only fooling."

"Look!" Norman turned the light on in a hurry. He reached
under his pillow, but the monsters had vanished. Even so,
he got up and threw the fake tooth out the window. And,
just to feel safe, he slept the rest of the night with the light on.

The next morning, Norman was tired
when he went to school. For the first time
in weeks, he didn't check his tooth.

At lunch, when he was eating his
peanut-butter-and-jelly sandwich,
Norman bit down on something hard.
It was his tooth. It had fallen out all by
itself—just like that. Just the way he had
always dreamed that it would happen.

"How will the tooth fairy hear that my tooth came out?" he asked his mother at bedtime.

"Don't worry," she said. "The tooth fairy knows all about it."

But Norman looked worried. "Suppose she isn't nice."

His mother patted him. "I'm sure she's someone you'd like."

Even so, Norman slept with the light on
again. He squeezed his eyes shut and
never opened them until morning.

When Norman felt under his pillow, sure enough, his tooth was gone. And in its place was a shiny new quarter.

Brush and Floss Your Teeth with Norman

1. With a twist of the wrist, use short gentle strokes to clean the outsides of teeth (upper and lower). Alternate this with a gentle circular motion where the teeth meet the gums.

2. With a twist of the wrist, brush the insides of back teeth (upper and lower). Alternate this with a circular motion where the teeth meet the gums.

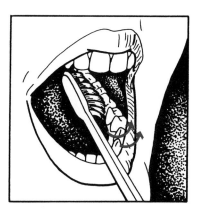

3. With a twist of the wrist, use quick gentle strokes with the tip of the brush on inside front of teeth (upper and lower). Alternate this with a circular motion where the teeth meet the gums.

4. Brush back and forth on the tops where you chew (upper and lower). Brush your teeth for two to three minutes. Try to brush after each meal, or at least after breakfast and dinner.

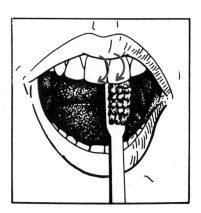

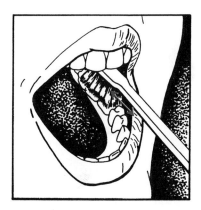

Flossing

1. Hold the floss like this.
2. Slide the floss gently between the teeth.
3. Gently scrape the sides of the tooth away from gums.

1.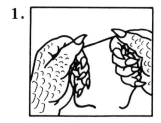

2.

3.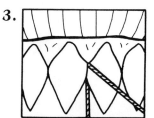

HOW NORMAN TAKES CARE
OF HIS TEETH

Bacteria, which are tiny germs, combine with food to make acids in your mouth. These acids dissolve the hard surface of your teeth. Whenever he can, Norman tries to brush his teeth very soon after eating sweets or starchy foods such as crackers to prevent tooth decay.

Norman cleans his teeth after breakfast and before he goes to bed. He uses a child-sized brush with soft, rounded bristles and a toothpaste containing fluoride. Norman spends two or three minutes carefully cleaning all the surfaces he can reach. Starting at the back of his mouth, he gently wiggles his brush from the gum toward the tips of his teeth. Then he scrubs the chewing surfaces. After brushing, Norman doesn't eat licorice, or any other food, before he goes to bed.

The bacteria in your mouth form an invisible sticky film called plaque. Norman uses dental floss every day to remove the plaque between his teeth and under his gums where his brush can't reach.

Norman visits his dentist regularly to keep his teeth healthy. Your dentist will tell you how you can use other forms of fluoride to fight decay-causing bacteria and keep your teeth strong.